Nobby
to Lap

by Darren & Julia Spence

This book belongs to:

Weird Grape
PUBLISHING

"Night night, Nobby!"

The Chocolate Labrador puppy settled down in his basket. His owner switched off the kitchen lights and shut the door. He heard the stairs creaking, and then it was quiet.

He should be going to sleep now. But Nobby was too excited to sleep. After all, it was Christmas Eve. He sniffed the air. Yes, there was a distinct whiff of Christmas magic.

It was a clear night, and the moon shone brightly through the kitchen window. Nobby looked across at the back door and the moonbeam falling on the dog flap.

He got out of his basket by the fire and crept across the shiny kitchen floor towards the door. He paused, wagged his tail with excitement then leapt through his dog flap.

Nobby flew through the air and made a very soft landing.

He was deep in snow.

It was very cold and it was dark. The moon shone from a blue-black sky filled with stars – more stars than Nobby had ever seen.

"Good morning!" said a voice in his ear.

Nobby jumped to his feet to see a dog with piercing blue eyes and the thickest coat of white fur.

"Good morning?" said Nobby. "What do you mean, good morning? It's the middle of the night. Look at all the stars!"

"Ah!" said the white dog. "A visitor. We don't usually get visitors on the big day itself. Still, now you're here ..."

"How do you know I'm a visitor?" said Nobby.

"Because otherwise," said the white dog, "you would know that here in the Arctic, it doesn't get light until nearly lunchtime. And then there's only a little bit of daylight before it gets dark again."

"This p-p-place is called the Arctic?" said Nobby, now shivering with cold.

"Well, we're in the Artic Circle," said the white dog, "but this is Lapland, which is of course the home of ..."

The dog stopped suddenly, her pale blue eyes resting on Nobby, who was quickly becoming frozen to the spot. A small icicle was forming on the end of his nose.

“I’m sorry, you’re not dressed for this weather. We huskies are used to it – special fur, you see. But you’ll need something to keep you warm. Come along.”

Nobby followed the white dog to a house that seemed to be made of logs. It was covered in snow and ice but a welcoming warm light shone through the windows.

Inside, they were greeted by a very cheerful lady with hair as white as the snow outside and rosy cheeks. "Naris! We wondered where you were. And who's the visitor?"

"I'm Nobby, and I'm from England!" barked Nobby.

Of course, the rosy-cheeked lady didn't understand any of this, but she did seem to understand exactly what the problem was.

"Poor love, you must be frozen," she said. "You'll need something to keep out the cold. Now I wonder what ..."

She starting searching the room, rummaging in all the drawers and cupboards. Eventually, she produced a large, red fur-lined hat.

“How about this? It’s one of the spares, so he won’t miss it.”

Nobby looked doubtfully at Naris. Surely he’d need more than a hat? And anyway, it would be far too big for him.

Then the rosy-cheeked lady did a strange thing. She took a pair of scissors from a drawer and started snipping holes in the hat.

“There we are!” she said, when she had finished. “Now all we have to do is pop your legs through the holes.”

Nobby found himself the proud wearer of a red, fur-lined coat.

It was a little baggy in places, but it was certainly cosy. Best of all though, his tail was snug and warm inside the end.

"Come on, Nobby," said Naris, heading for the door. "It's not long now until take-off, and there's work to do before then. We need to go and check on the reindeer."

Nobby followed, somewhat confused. What did she mean, take off? Reindeer? Why check on reindeer?

Outside, day had dawned, and a frosty sunlight was streaming through the trees.

Nobby followed Naris round to the side of the log house where there was a large stable. And there, sure enough, was a small herd of reindeer, tucking into piles of hay and carrots. Nobby recognised the animals from the cards and decorations in his home. Parked next to the stable was an enormous sleigh.

"They're stocking up, ready for tonight - they're going to be busy," said Naris. "I'll just check they're all there."

Naris nodded as she counted each pair of antlers. Then she turned to Nobby with an urgent look.

"Only eight! There's one missing. We'll have to go and look for it."

The two dogs set off in search of the missing reindeer.

"It's probably just wandered off," said Naris. "I expect it headed towards the forest."

Nobby tried to keep up with Naris, but it wasn't easy. What with his short legs and the deep snow and the hat bunching around his knees, he really couldn't move very fast. And as Naris got further away, it became more and more difficult to see her white shape against the snowy white landscape.

After a few minutes, Nobby looked up and realised that he couldn't see the white shape at all.

"Naris!" he called. His voice echoed. Then silence.

Nobby wondered what he should do now. The best thing, he thought, would be to try and find his way back to the house.

As he looked around trying to get his bearings, he noticed a little way ahead a trail of footprints in the snow. Naris's tracks! Well, all he had to do now was follow the trail.

Nobby set off once more, keeping his nose very close to the ground.

The tracks wandered this way and that …

… round and round …

... in and out of the fir trees ...

… and eventually led the way to …

… some long, brown, furry legs.

Nobby looked up to see a bright red nose
and a large pair of antlers.

It was all very well finding the missing reindeer. But what was he going to do now?

"Naris! - Naaaa-ris!" Nobby sent a forlorn cry through the still frosty air, with little hope of a reply.

But then, in the distance, came a faint bark.

"Nooo - bby?"

A few seconds later, Naris bounded up in a flurry of snow.

"Nobby! Well done! Now, let's get him back."

As they turned round to make their way back to the log cabin, Nobby stared in amazement.

The twilight sky was full of coloured patterns, leaping up and down like flames.

"It's the Northern Lights," explained Naris. "They sometimes appear in the sky here in winter."

They watched for a few moments, entranced by the beautiful dancing beams of light.

Naris shook herself. “It’s getting dark,” she said. “He’ll be setting off soon. Come on, we’ve no time to lose.”

Naris and Nobby gently herded the reindeer back to the log house. When they arrived, Nobby saw that the other reindeer were now harnessed to the sleigh. As the runaway reindeer went over to join them, a deep voice boomed from the stable, “Ah, Rudolph! Where have you been? Come along, now – we’re nearly ready to go.”

As they stood by the stable, Nobby shivered. He suddenly realised that despite the fur-lined hat he was now feeling quite chilly. Naris looked at him anxiously.

"Nobby, why don't you go into the house and warm up? I'll be there in a few minutes."

Nobby nodded gratefully and padded off to the house.

Inside, the rosy-cheeked lady was busy by the oven. She didn't notice Nobby as he crept through the door and onto a chair by the crackling fire.

Nobby tucked his nose inside the fur-lined hat, enjoying the warmth of the log cabin. His mind drifted back to the beautiful Northern Lights. A few minutes later, he was so fast asleep that he didn't even hear the door open.

"We're off now, dear. Brrrgh! I think it's even colder than usual this year. Think I'll take a spare hat, just in case. Ah, here we are …"

A large hand whisked the fur-lined hat and its sleeping occupant off the chair.

When Nobby woke up he could feel that he was moving. It was a bit like being in a car, only smoother. And what was that noise? It sounded like jingling bells. And there was another sound, like rushing wind.

Then he remembered falling asleep in front of the fire. So, where was he now? Cautiously, he poked his head out of the hat.

Nobby gasped as he took in the view, things began to make sense. Here he was in an enormous sleigh being pulled by a herd of reindeer. On the seat beside him was a large bearded gentleman dressed in a red cloak with white fur. Behind him were hundreds of red sacks. The blue-black sky above was full of twinkling stars, and the ground below … well, the ground was a very, very long way below. Nobby felt on top of the world but kept quiet in case he was seen.

Nobby's eyes were heavy. It had been a very exciting day for the little puppy. The movement of the sleigh soon rocked him into a deep sleep.

“Merry Christmas Nobby! ”

Nobby’s owner came bounding downstairs and into the kitchen.

“Nobby? Where are you?”

She stood by his basket with a puzzled look on her face. There was no sign of the cheeky little puppy, only a Father Christmas hat – curiously full of holes.

A muffled bark came from under the tree. The presents began to move.

“Nobby?”

Nobby’s sleepy head appeared.

“Nobby! What are you doing under there?”

Nobby wriggled out and wagged his tail, he had a bow stuck to his head and tinsel trailing behind him.

"Oh Nobby, what could be a nicer Christmas present than you!"

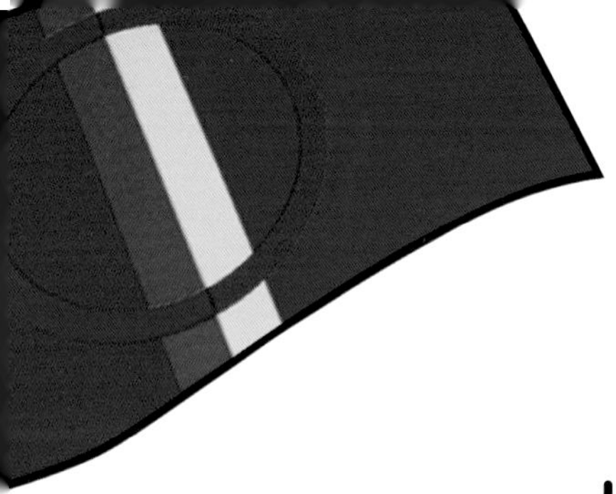

Facts about **Lapland** ...

Money:	**€ Euro**
Featured Dog:	**Siberian Husky**
Famous Resident:	**Father Christmas**
Flying Time from London, England:	**3 Hours**

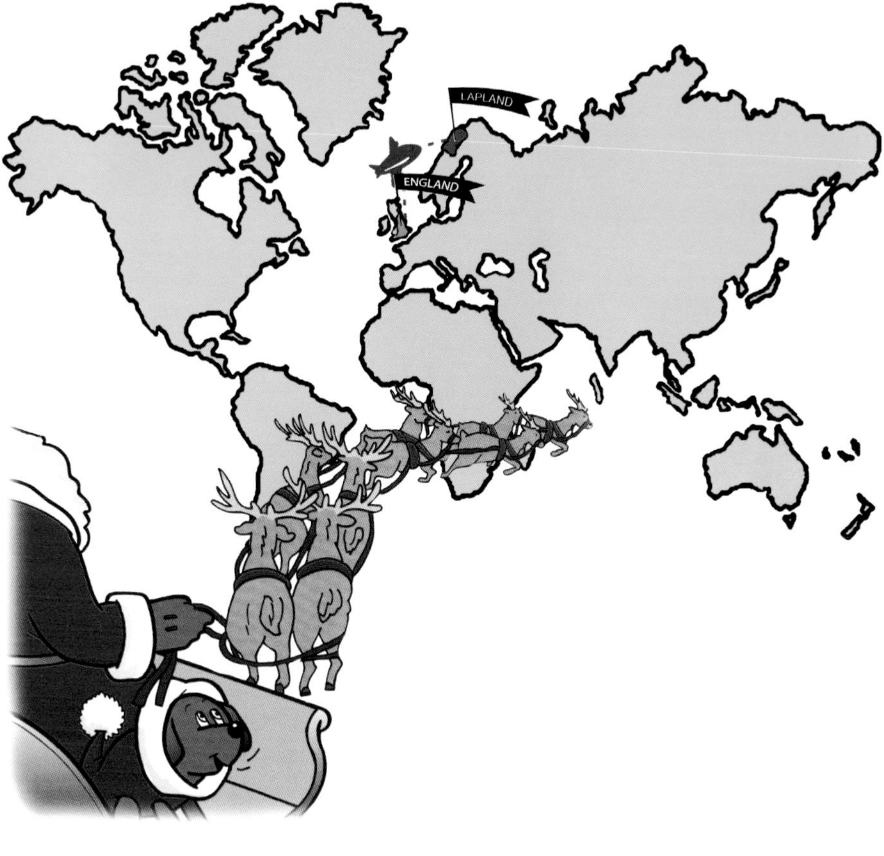
LAPLAND
ENGLAND

Become a Nobby Traveller !

If you enjoyed this "Nobby Travels" story, why not join our exclusive members club and become a Nobby Traveller? When you join, you'll receive:

- **a Nobby Traveller passport to record your travels**
- **a Nobby Traveller bag**
- **a set of Nobby Travels stickers**
- **Money-off vouchers**

... **plus**, you'll have access to the members-only area of the Nobby Travels website, where you can:

- **download loads of cool stuff**
- **take part in competitions**
- **keep up to date with news about Nobby**

To become a Nobby Traveller, simply visit **www.nobbytravels.com/nobbytraveller**

All for just £5 per year